WITHDRAWN

TOKI
"The Cobalt Kingdom"

GRIMBO (E)
"Moss Ocean"

SALASSANDRA
"Mystic's Moon"

MON DOMANI
"Mother World"

The Praise for 5 Worlds Is Out of This World!

"A bang-zoom start to a series that promises to be epic
in both the classical and internet senses of the word."
—*The New York Times Book Review*

"For kids who love fantasy and other-world adventures,
and for any fans of graphic novels, this book is a must-read."
—R. J. Palacio, #1 *New York Times* bestselling author of *Wonder*

★ "Sensitive writing, gorgeous artwork, and riveting plot,
this is a series to keep an eye on."
—*Booklist*, Starred Review

★ "A dazzling interplanetary fantasy . . . that will easily appeal
to fans of *Naruto* or *Avatar: The Last Airbender*."
—*Publishers Weekly*, Starred Review

"Plenty of adventure as truths are uncovered . . .
Give to fans of Judd Winick's Hilo or Kazu Kibuishi's Amulet series."
—*School Library Journal*

"Epic action, adventure, and mystery will draw you in, but the heartfelt characters
and their seemingly impossible journey will keep you turning the pages."
—Lisa Yee, author of the DC Super Hero Girls™ series

5 Worlds

BOOK 3

THE RED MAZE

Mark
SIEGEL

Alexis
SIEGEL

Xanthe
BOUMA

Boya
SUN

Matt
ROCKEFELLER

Random House 🏠 New York

"Many deaths, and many births,
Windows in and windows out."
—Ancient Felid carving, translation uncertain

JAX ON SALASSANDRA

5

THE SALASSI DEVOTI

AND I MET THE *SALASSI DEVOTI.*

BZZT--LIGHT THE BEACONS.

JUST WANTED-- *BZZT*--

TO SERVE A TRUE PURPOSE-- *BZZT.*

DID YOU HEAR THAT?

WAS IT INVOLVED IN LIGHTING THE *DOMANI BEACON?*

IMPOSSIBLE.

BUT THIS IS NO HUMAN. IT'S A *MACHINE.*

YOU ARE CORRECT. BUT I *YEARNED* FOR THAT TO CHANGE.

MACHINES DON'T FEEL *YEARNING!*

WE ARE *FADING AWAY.* NO MACHINE IS GOING TO HELP THAT.

I DREAMED OF SEEING *THE OTHER BEACONS LIT.*

YES.

UNCLE JEP BUILT ME AROUND A--*BZZT*--*QUANTUM VACANCY.* I ASKED HIM ONCE WHY HE PUT--*BZZT*--*EMPTINESS* IN MY MIDDLE.

"IN HONOR OF MY OWN MAKER."

AND WHAT DID HE SAY?

I HOPE YOU'RE NOT THINKING WHAT I THINK YOU'RE THINKING, *ESKE.*

WELL, ISN'T THAT WHY WE CAN'T *ATTEND* HUMANS ANYMORE? THEY'RE *TOO FULL*--NO *ROOM* FOR US ANY LONGER.

THEY'RE FULL OF THINGS WE CAN'T *LIVE* WITH.

MAYBE *THIS* IS OUR LAST CHANCE!

NO, THANK YOU. IT'S NO HOME FOR THE *DEVOTI.* I'D SOONER *DISSOLVE INTO WIND.*

NOT I.

THAT *VACANCY*-- THAT MIGHT EXPLAIN YOUR YEARNING, *MACHINE MAN.*

MY NAME IS *JAX.*

THE VACANCY IS HELD IN *STELLAR CONDENSATE MILK* THAT RUNS THROUGH MY NANO-CIRCUITRY.

HUH?

NEVER MIND. I'M BROKEN.

I CAN'T EVEN ACCESS MY *DIAGNOSTICS.* I'M-- *BZZT*--FADING AWAY, LIKE YOU. *SYSTEMS FAILING--BZZT--*

ONE BY ONE.

FROM THAT SPACE IN THE MIDDLE OF YOU, I COULD ACCESS YOUR *INNER WORKINGS*, COULDN'T I?

ESKE! YOU'RE NOT GIVING YOURSELF UP TO A *ROBOT!*

A HOME IS A HOME.

"MANY DEATHS, AND MANY BIRTHS," AS THE POEM GOES. *THE TIME OF THE BEACONS* IS UPON US.

I'M DONE *RETREATING.* WE ARE NEEDED IN THE WORLDS!

A FEW DAYS LATER I REACHED A SMALL VILLAGE...

AMBEROON.

AFTER ASKING AROUND, I WAS DIRECTED TO *O'ZIRG'S* SHOP.

LET'S START WITH THIS FINE *DOMANI* OUTFIT--

I LIKE THAT ONE.

SIMPLE, BUT NICE.

HE TOLD ME THAT THE CAPTAINS OF THE *FLITORI HAD NOT* BETRAYED US...

...THAT IT WAS ALL A MISUNDERSTANDING.

YES, I GUESS IT IS LIKE THAT....

YOU'VE CHANGED TOO, OONA.

PLIP

I'M STILL NOT USED TO SEEING YOU AS *TOKI*.

ME NEITHER, HONESTLY. IT ALL HAPPENED SO SUDDENLY.

I FORGET SOMETIMES, THEN I'M STARTLED BY *MY OWN REFLECTION*.

YOU *HAD* TO DO IT, RIGHT? TO PRETEND YOU WERE GOING ALONG WITH *THE COBALT PRINCE'S* PLAN?

THAT WAS PART OF IT.

BUT IN AMONG HIS *LIES*, THE PRINCE WAS TELLING THE *TRUTH* ABOUT MY SISTER AND ME.

WE WERE BORN *TOKI*. AND WE HAD BEEN *ALTERED*.

THE PRINCE WAS *CORRUPTED* BY THE *MIMIC*, BUT I STILL LEARNED A LOT FROM HIM.

I'M SORRY I GOT SO ANGRY WHEN I SAW YOU CHANGED. *I HATED THE TOKI FOR ATTACKING MON DOMANI....*

I KNOW.

JUMP

ha ha!

SPLASH

SPLOOSH

WERE YOU ABLE TO TALK TO YOUR SISTER BEFORE SHE DIED?

NOT ENOUGH. JUST THAT ONE NIGHT IN THE PRISON.

SHE REALIZED SHE'D BEEN TRICKED INTO FOLLOWING THE PRINCE.

I *THOUGHT* WE'D HAVE MANY MORE CHANCES TO MAKE UP FOR ALL OUR YEARS APART.

BUT WHEN IT LOOKED LIKE THE *MIMIC* HAD *WON...*

JESSA GAVE HER LIFE TO SEAL THE MIMIC'S HEART IN MOLTEN GLASS!

THE LAST THING SHE SAID TO ME WAS *"SISTERS ARE FOREVER!"*

SNIF!

JAX...?

OONA NEEDS US. SHE CAN'T LIGHT THE BEACONS ALONE.

THEY SHOWED ME *A SAND CLOCK*. TIME IS RUNNING OUT....

I FELT LIKE I'D SEEN ALL THIS BEFORE.

BZZZZTT!!

HELLO? CAN YOU JOIN US ON THE BRIDGE?

OONA IS ALL OVER THE *CITIZEN FEEDS.*

OH WAIT! ANOTHER MESSAGE. GOVERNMENT CHANNEL...

"OONA LEE, JAX AMBOY, AND THEIR ENTOURAGE ARE INVITED TO LAND...

...AT *THE GARNET PALACE!"*

OONA, YOU'RE FAMOUS!

HOW ABOUT A MORE *DISCREET* ENTRANCE? LANDING IN THE SOUTHERN DESERT?

TIME IS RUNNING OUT. I NEED TO GO STRAIGHT TO THE *RED BEACON!*

IT'S **MOON YATTA**! WE'RE IN THE **FREE** WORLD HERE!

WE DON'T NEED TO WORRY ABOUT AN **EVIL TOKI PRINCE.**

MOON YATTA HAS PROBLEMS OF ITS OWN.

SURE, BUT THEY **ELECT** THEIR LEADERS! "MOON YATTA, LAND OF HOPES AND DREAMS COME TRUE!"

THE **MIMIC** IS HERE TOO. WE'RE SEEING SIGNS OF IT EVERYWHERE.

BUT THE **MIMIC** LOST ITS HEART ON TOKI!

THAT DIDN'T DESTROY IT.

WE'RE STARTING OUR DESCENT. COMING IN OVER THE OUTLANDS FIRST.

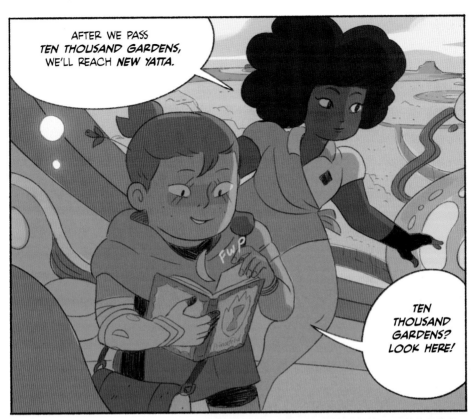

AFTER WE PASS *TEN THOUSAND GARDENS*, WE'LL REACH *NEW YATTA*.

FWP

TEN THOUSAND GARDENS? LOOK HERE!

THE LAST THING I HAVE OF MY DAD'S.

GROW TALL at... 10,000 GARDENS

IF ONLY HE COULD SEE IT WITH ME.

IT HAS CHANGED.

I DON'T UNDERSTAND-- WHERE ARE THE *YATTA FARMLANDS*?

"THE COUNTLESS FRUIT FOR THE GALAXY"?

STAN MOON BOUGHT THEM ALL.... "ONE CROP TO FEED ALL PEOPLE."

WHAT'S THE MATTER, *AN TZU*?

STAN MOON, INC.! THEY BOUGHT UP MOST OF THE MON DOMANI LANDS.

WE ENDED UP IN SAO SABLO WITH NOTHING TO EAT BUT THAT DISGUSTING ORANGE SPRAY.

MY DAD WOULDN'T SELL, SO THEY SHUT US OUT OF THE MARKETS AND WE LOST THE FAMILY FARM!

YES, STAN MOON AND THE BIG YATTAN CORPORATIONS SEEM TO RUN THE SHOW. THE GOVERNMENTS DON'T STAND UP TO THEM.

HERE ON YATTA THEY OVERTURNED THE LAWS PROTECTING THE AIR AND WATER AND SOIL!

WE SHOULD SHOW THEM WHAT HAPPENED TO LAKE EDENIU.

THE WATER HAS BEEN DIVERTED TO IRRIGATE *THE STAN MOON FIELDS.*

WHICH SPEEDS UP THE PLANET'S *OVERHEATING.*

46

LOOK AT THAT *STARBALL STADIUM!*

JAX, DO YOU MISS PLAYING?

NO...

YES, MAYBE A LITTLE.

MY *TEAMMATES...* IT WOULD BE NICE TO SEE THE *AMBER LEATHERHEADS* AGAIN. THE TEAM OWNER, *DERRICK STOAK...*

I THINK HE WAS... *PROUD* OF US? BUT I WAS HIS *MACHINE--* HIS *BEST* MACHINE.

YOU'RE *MORE* THAN A MACHINE NOW!

MY DAD USED TO TELL THIS JOKE....

A CITY MAN IS LOST AND ASKS A *DOMANI* FARMER FOR DIRECTIONS TO *CHRYSALIS.*

THE FARMER SAYS, "SURE, GO BACK TO THE CROSSING.... OR NO, TAKE THAT VALLEY ROAD....

OH NO, THAT WON'T WORK EITHER...."

THE FARMER THINKS AND THINKS.... AND FINALLY HE SAYS--

"THE BEST WAY TO GET THERE IS...TO NOT START FROM HERE!"

HA HA!

HE HE

WAIT. DOES THAT EVEN MAKE SENSE?

Chapter 2
THE GARNET PALACE

52

PHEW! IT'S ALL TOO MUCH! CAN'T I JUST GO STRAIGHT TO THE BEACON?

SLAM

AT LEAST EVERYONE SEEMS HAPPY TO SEE YOU!

ARE THEY?

I REMEMBER THE *HEAD CITIZEN.* I MET HER EVERY TIME MY TEAM WON *THE INTERWORLD SERIES.*

STURRITZ

REALLY?

WHAT WAS SHE LIKE?

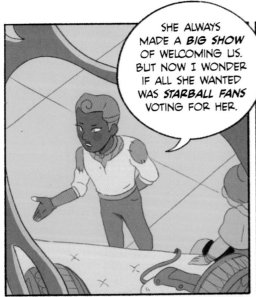

SHE ALWAYS MADE A *BIG SHOW* OF WELCOMING US. BUT NOW I WONDER IF ALL SHE WANTED WAS *STARBALL FANS* VOTING FOR HER.

PEOPLE IN POWER ALWAYS HAVE *THE NEXT CAMPAIGN* TO THINK ABOUT. AND WE'RE IN THE MIDDLE OF *ELECTION SEASON.*

SO SHE MAY NOT CARE ABOUT *LIGHTING BEACONS.*

PROBABLY NOT.

THEY'LL BE SERVING *REAL* FOOD, RIGHT?

REELECT STURRITZ

OH, LOOK, SHE'S *THAT DOMANI DANCER* WHO LIT THE BEACON. ISN'T SHE *CUTE?*

YES, SO "COUNTRY" IN *TOKI BLUE.* AND THAT *KID* FROM THE SLUMS. JUST ADORABLE.

A FEW NANO-COSMETIC TOUCHES WOULD DO *WONDERS* ON HER.

I HEAR THIS YEAR IT'S GOING TO BE ALL ABOUT *LONG NECKS.*

56

FROM *MINTZ!*

PROBABLY THE *BEST* RESTAURANT IN THE FIVE WORLDS!

FROM *GRIMBO (E)?*

MMMM. YOU GOTTA TRY THIS!

LEAVE SOME FOR THE REST OF US....

IMPRESSIVE, ISN'T IT?

NOT AS SPECTACULAR, I'M SURE, AS SOME OF THE SAND DANCES YOU'VE DONE, *OONA...*

WE USED TO HAVE *FANTASTIC* SHOWS, UNLIKE ANYTHING ON ANY WORLD...BACK WHEN THE *SHAPESHIFTERS* WERE ALLOWED TO DO THEIR *TRANSFORMING DANCES.*

WELL, ABOUT THAT, I WANTED TO ASK YOU--

RIGHT, BRIGHTLEY?

INDEED.

...

EXCUSE ME, I'LL BE RIGHT BACK.

DID SHE JUST SAY *SHAPE-SHIFTERS?*

YES, AN ANCIENT PEOPLE, THE FIRST *YATTANS.* THEY HAVE ABILITIES TO...

...*TRANSFORM.*

BUT THEY'RE NOT ALLOWED TO DO *THEIR OWN DANCES?*

NO, THEY'RE NO LONGER *ALLOWED* TO TRANSFORM AT ALL. NOT IN THE URBAN AREAS, AT LEAST.

YOU SEE THE *STATUE?*

WHY NOT?

IT CELEBRATES *THE BATTLE OF THE RED BEACON.*

THAT'S WHEN THE FIRST YATTANS SURRENDERED THE BEACON.... AFTER THAT, *TRANSFORMING DANCES* BECAME ILLEGAL. PEOPLE WERE AFRAID, YOU SEE.

LONG STORY.

SO WHERE ARE THESE *SHAPESHIFTERS* NOW?

MOSTLY STILL HERE, BUT THEY HAVE TO WEAR *FORM-LOCK COLLARS.*

THE ONES WHO REFUSE HIDE IN *THE RUBY DESERT.* THEY FACE *ARREST* IF THEY ENTER ANY POPULATED AREA.

ARREST? FOR BEING SHAPESHIFTERS? ON *MOON YATTA,* LAND OF FREEDOM AND DREAMS?

HAVE OUR GUESTS BEEN ENJOYING THEMSELVES, *BRIGHTLEY?*

PLEASE UNDERSTAND, *MISS LEE*, THE HEAD CITIZEN HAS A LOT ON HER MIND WITH THE CURRENT ELECTION....

WHAT ABOUT SAVING THE *FIVE WORLDS*? ISN'T THAT MORE IMPORTANT?

I DO ADMIRE YOUR PASSION, *MISS LEE.*

EVEN AT A BETTER TIME, THE HEAD CITIZEN...MAY NOT BE *THE RIGHT PERSON* TO SPEAK TO...ABOUT ACCESS TO THE BEACON...

IF I MAY...

REALLY?

THE FACILITIES AROUND THE BEACON BELONG TO *NANOTEX CORPORATION.* THE OWNERS OF THAT COMPANY ARE THE ONES YOU SHOULD SPEAK TO.

WHO ARE THEY?

ELDRIDGE AND DERRICK STOAK. I KNOW THEM WELL. DERRICK OWNS *THE AMBER LEATHERHEADS.*

RAM SAM SAM, MY FRIEND, WHEN WE GO LIGHT THAT *GREEN BEACON,* WE'VE GOT TO HAVE A MEAL AT *MINTZ.* MMM, THAT SEAWEED!

YEOUCH!

TRIP!!

AN TZU!!

I'VE GOT YOU.

I'M ALL RIGHT. I'M ALL RIGHT!

IS IT TRUE *YATTA* HAS THE BEST DOCTORS?

ABSOLUTELY. I'LL ASK *FELIZIA'S* PERSONAL DOCTOR TO SEE HIM!

THANK YOU SO MUCH, MR. *BRIGHTLEY.*

YES, THANK YOU.

NO NEED TO THANK ME. *SUCCEEDING* IN YOUR MISSION WILL BE QUITE ENOUGH THANKS, *LIGHTER OF BEACONS.*

LIGHT IT, OONA LEE.

LIGHT THE BEACON BEFORE IT'S TOO LATE!

I... YES... THAT'S WHY I'M HERE.

AND IT'S AN ABSOLUTE OUTRAGE THAT--

THE PEET BO

THE *GOOD* NEWS IS, YOU'VE COME TO THE RIGHT PLACE, AND TO *THE RIGHT DOCTOR!*

THAT'S GREAT! YOU'LL BE ABLE TO HELP?

I'M CONFIDENT I WILL!

SO YOU'VE TREATED CASES LIKE THIS BEFORE?

NOT EXACTLY. THIS "VANISHING ILLNESS" IS VERY UNUSUAL.

SO YOU DON'T KNOW WHAT IT IS.

WE HAVE THE LATEST *TECHNOLOGY!* OUR INVESTIGATIVE TOOLS ARE SECOND TO NONE.

WE ISOLATE THE CAUSE, AND THE COURSE OF TREATMENT FOLLOWS JUST LIKE THAT!

WHEN CAN WE START?

AS SOON AS THE *FINANCIALS* ARE TAKEN CARE OF!

THE... FINANCIALS?

YES, MY FEE IS *3,000* YATTAN CREDITS....

LET'S SEE, 10...

15, 20 DOMANI...

THAT'S OVER 10,000 DOMANI CREDITS!

YES, 3,000 *PER STANDARD HOUR.*

WAIT. 3,000?!

PER HOUR?!

TO START, WE'LL NEED TO SET ASIDE *A WEEK* FOR THE TESTS AND FIRST TREATMENTS.

WE DON'T HAVE THAT MUCH--

WHOA, WHOA, WHOA-- BRIGHTLEY NEVER SAID HE WAS SENDING ME *A CHARITY CASE!*

I UNDERSTAND, IT'S JUST THAT WE--

YOU'RE A DOCTOR! AREN'T YOU IN THE *HEALING* BUSINESS FIRST?

WE'RE *DONE* HERE. *HOSPITAL POLICY.* NOTHING I CAN DO, I'M AFRAID. I HAVE A FAMILY TO FEED, YOU KNOW.

SLAM!

GO ON AHEAD. I'LL MEET YOU OUTSIDE.

THIS PLACE ISN'T THE *MOON YATTA* MY DAD DREAMED ABOUT.

WHAT'S THAT BAG, JAX?

I FOUND THEIR *PROSTHETICS* DEPARTMENT.

BUT... DID YOU... STEAL IT?

WE CAME HERE TO GET HELP FOR MY FRIEND *AN TZU.*

THIS HELPS!

WOW.

Chapter 4

THE STOAK BROTHER

ARE YOU SURE, *OONA?* I STILL THINK I SHOULD GO WITH YOU. I'M... WORRIED.

THEY'LL WANT YOU BACK ON THE TEAM.

YEAH, FOR *THE BIG GAME.* I WOULD HAVE KILLED TO SEE *THAT,* NOT SO LONG AGO....

I *NEED* TO DO IT. THIS MIGHT BE THE ONLY WAY I CAN GET TO THE *RED BEACON.*

IF HE EVEN GRANTS YOU ACCESS TO IT... HE'LL DEMAND SOMETHING IN RETURN. I KNOW *DERRICK STOAK.*

HIS *STARBALL CHAMPION.*

I'LL DO IT.

JAX, NO! LET ME TALK TO HIM. HE AGREED TO SEE ME. MAYBE HE'LL DO THE RIGHT THING.

HE'LL WANT *JAX AMBOY* BACK ON THE LEATHERHEADS.

I'LL SEE YOU BACK AT THE GARNET PALACE.

DERRICK STOAK, DO THE RIGHT THING? I DOUBT IT.

NAN TEX
DERRICK STOAK

YOU REALLY LIT THE *DOMANI BEACON?*

I DID.

BUT YOU FAILED TO LIGHT THE BLUE ONE ON *TOKI.*

YES.

AND YOU THINK YOU CAN LIGHT THE RED BEACON OF *MOON YATTA.*

EXACTLY. BUT IT'S COVERED IN ALL THESE *PIPES* AND THINGS. I CAN'T GET TO IT.

AND WHY SHOULD I HELP YOU DO THAT?

EXCUSE ME?

WHY SHOULD I HELP YOU?

WHILE THE OTHER WORLDS WERE BUSY SINGING *LEGENDS* ABOUT THE BEACONS, WE FOUND A WAY TO *HARNESS* THE POWER OF *OUR* BEACON.

WITH UNLIMITED ENERGY, *MOON YATTA* HAS BECOME THE *MOST ADVANCED* OF THE FIVE WORLDS.

WHY WOULD WE WANT TO *THREATEN* THAT BY LETTING YOU LIGHT THE RED BEACON?

BECAUSE YOUR WORLD IS *OVERHEATING*, LIKE THE OTHERS.

BEING THE MOST ADVANCED OF FIVE *DEAD* WORLDS IS NO GREAT PRIZE.

HOW DO YOU KNOW LIGHTING THE BEACONS WILL SOLVE THE PROBLEM?

YES, RAIN CAME TO *MON DOMANI* AFTER YOU LIT THE WHITE ONE...

BUT NOW THEY'RE FACING *FLOODS.* SO WHAT MAKES YOU SO SURE YOU'RE HELPING?

AND PLEASE DON'T QUOTE *FELID TEXTS*--

I DON'T NEED TO.

I MET *PROFESSOR ETTO.* HE TOLD ME ABOUT HIS RESEARCH ON THE BEACONS.

A CHANCE TO DO RIGHT. AND PLAY YOUR PART IN SAVING THE WORLDS FROM EXTINCTION.

HOW TOUCHING. YOU'LL HAVE TO DO BETTER THAN THAT, *MISS LEE.* I'M A BUSINESSMAN, NOT AN *IDEALIST.*

I THINK YOU KNOW WHAT I WANT.

PROFESSOR *ETTO'S* "NEPHEW." I BELIEVE YOU KNOW HIS LITTLE SECRET.

YES, I DO.

SO YOU'RE READY TO RETURN MY ANDROID TO ME?

HE'S CHANGED, *MR. STOAK.* HE'S NOT JUST AN ANDROID.

I KNOW! HE'S SO MUCH MORE! I MADE HIM INTO A *STAR*!

NO, NO, THIS IS SOMETHING ELSE, MR. STOAK.

A *SALASSI SPIRIT LIFE* JOINED HIM.

HE'S... HE'S A *REAL PERSON* NOW.

YOU DIDN'T SEEM LIKE THE *GULLIBLE* TYPE.

CLEARLY YOU WERE TAKEN IN BY SOME CLEVER REPROGRAMMING.... YOU WANT THE BEACON? *I WANT MY STARBALL CHAMPION.*

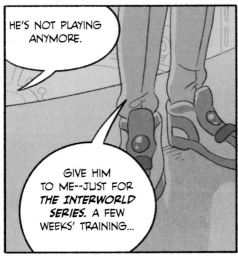

HE'S NOT PLAYING ANYMORE.

GIVE HIM TO ME--JUST FOR *THE INTERWORLD SERIES.* A FEW WEEKS' TRAINING...

...A FEW GAMES. AND *THE BEACON'S ALL YOURS* TO DO YOUR *SAND DANCING THING.*

HOW DO I KNOW YOU'LL KEEP YOUR WORD?

YOU HAVE TO TRUST ME. I FOLLOW THROUGH ON MY DEALS.

I HOPE SO.

I'LL TALK TO *JAX,* BUT IT'S *HIS* DECISION.

YOU DON'T BELIEVE ME, BUT JAX IS MORE THAN A MACHINE.

MR. STOAK?

YES?

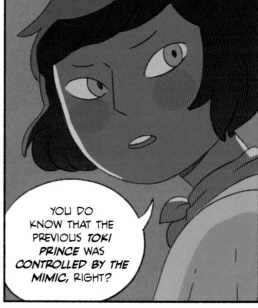

YOU DO KNOW THAT THE PREVIOUS *TOKI PRINCE* WAS *CONTROLLED BY THE MIMIC,* RIGHT?

OH, DON'T TELL ME YOU BELIEVE THOSE *OLD WIVES' TALES* ABOUT THE...

THE MIMIC...

I SAW IT WITH MY OWN EYES. WHAT IT DOES TO PEOPLE, HOW IT TAKES THEM OVER.

WHY ARE YOU TELLING ME THIS?

IT'S HERE ON *MOON YATTA* TOO. CLOSER THAN YOU THINK.

IF YOU CARE ABOUT YOUR HOME WORLD, YOU'LL HELP ME.

Chapter 5
SYSTEM OVERRIDES

88

I DON'T LIKE IT, *ELDRIDGE.*

WHY IS *STAN MOON* TAKING THE SPOTLIGHT LIKE THIS?

YOU DON'T GET IT, *DERRICK.* STICK TO *STARBALL,* BROTHER, AND LET *ME* HANDLE POLITICS.

BUT WE DON'T NEED *STAN MOON!*

NANOTEX IS KING! WHY ARE WE BOWING AND SCRAPING TO... THAT *THING?* WHATEVER IT IS.

IT'S A *SMART ALLIANCE.* TRUST ME. I CAN WORK WITH HIM, LET HIM FEEL LIKE HE'S IN CHARGE. HE RELIES ON ME.

AT THE RIGHT TIME, *NANOTEX* WILL TAKE OVER *STAN MOON,* AND WE WON'T NEED HIM ANYMORE.

HE'S...

THERE'S SOMETHING *NOT RIGHT.*

MEANWHILE...

GOTTA FIND A WAY *IN.*

THERE'S A WALKWAY *HERE!*

UP THERE?

THIS WHOLE PLACE IS *BUZZING.*

RAM SAM SAM DOESN'T SEEM TO LIKE IT.

BLIP!

MAPPING IS HARDER AND HARDER. I THINK *THAT WAY* IS THE CORE.

JAX, YOU BELIEVE *STOAK* WILL KEEP HIS WORD? WE CAN'T RISK LOSING YOU AGAIN!

YOU *WON'T* LOSE ME. DERRICK MAY BE LYING. BUT EVEN IF HE IS, I'LL FIND A WAY TO STAY TRUE TO MYSELF. AND TO MY FRIENDS.

I'LL OFFER TO PLAY THE *INTERWORLD GAME*...

IF HE'LL LET YOU GET TO THE *BEACON*.

BE CAREFUL, JAX!

YOU TOO, OONA.

blorp blp

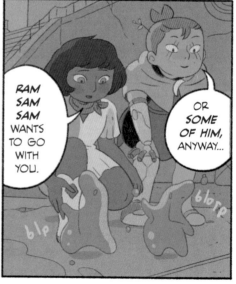

RAM SAM SAM WANTS TO GO WITH YOU.

OR *SOME* OF HIM, ANYWAY...

blp blorp

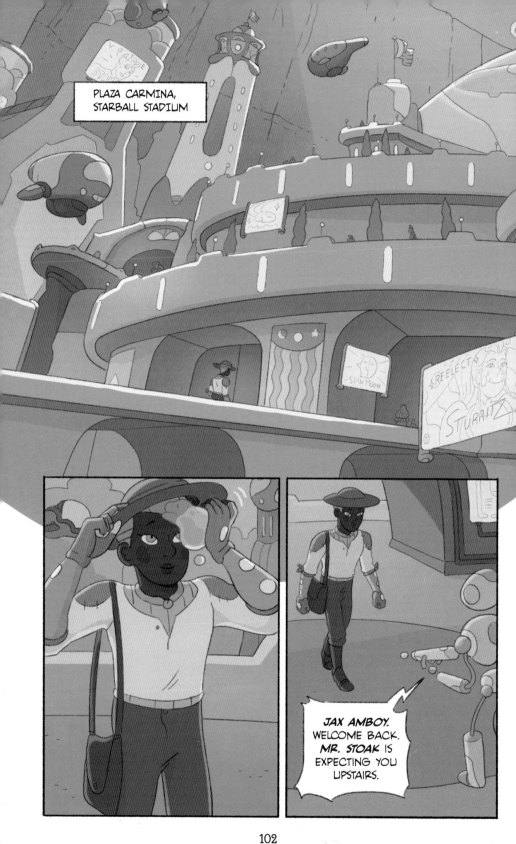

PLAZA CARMINA,
STARBALL STADIUM

JAX AMBOY.
WELCOME BACK.
MR. STOAK IS
EXPECTING YOU
UPSTAIRS.

THANK YOU, MR. STOAK.

IT'S OKAY TO CALL ME DERRICK NOW.

AFTER ALL THAT NASTY *TOKI* BUSINESS ON *MON DOMANI*, I THOUGHT YOU WERE TOTALLED!

NO INTERNAL DAMAGE, RIGHT?

NO, DERRICK.

GOOD, GOOD. WHAT'S WITH THE FINGERS?

PROFESSOR ETTO HAD TO MAKE A FEW REPAIRS. I LOST MY ARM IN THE STADIUM WRECKAGE. THIS WAS ALL HE HAD.

CRAZY OLD ETTO. TOO BAD HE CAN'T SEE YOUR COMEBACK GAME!

IT'S GOING TO BE *MONUMENTAL!* WE'LL BEAM LIVE ON *ALL WORLDS!*

THE GAME IS *SCHEDULED* ALREADY?

THE *LEATHERHEADS ARE BACK!* WAIT TILL YOUR TEAMMATES HEAR!

WHEN YOU DISAPPEARED, *TWYPSEN* TOOK IT HARD. THEY ALL DID.

LETOKO EVEN TALKED ABOUT RETIRING.

TWYPSEN! GOOD OLD TWYPSEN...

NOW THEY'VE GOT A NEW *INTERWORLD SERIES TROPHY* TO LOOK FORWARD TO!

YOU PROMISED *OONA LEE* YOU'D GIVE HER ACCESS TO THE BEACON IF I PLAY IN THE INTERWORLDS.

THAT SAND DANCER?

SHE'S A LOOSE CANNON, THAT ONE.

MY BROTHER IS HARDLY GOING TO LET HER *LIGHT THE THING,* IS HE?

WE DON'T EVEN KNOW WHAT COULD HAPPEN.

WHAT IF IT OVERLOADS MOON YATTA'S POWER GRID? NO, THERE'S NO WAY SHE'S GOING *ANYWHERE NEAR* THE RED BEACON.

YOU LIED TO HER! YOU LIED!

HOW COULD YOU DO SUCH A THING?

SLAM!

HUFF HF...

SOMETHING REALLY DID HAPPEN TO YOU.

YES! IF YOU WANT AN OBEDIENT ROBOT, BUILD YOURSELF A NEW ONE.

NO BEACON, NO GAME. WE DON'T HAVE A DEAL.

GENERAL SYSTEM OVERRIDE. CORE DIRECTIVE J-A-X, VOICE ACTIVATED-- DERRICK STOAK!

REPEAT, DERRICK STOAK.

CORE DIRECTIVE ACKNOWLEDGED. AWAITING FURTHER INSTRUCTIONS.

CALDEN, TIME FOR YOU TO WORK ON OUR LITTLE PROJECT AGAIN.

YES, JAX AMBOY IS BACK.

BUT HE'S BEEN MESSED WITH.

THE ACTIVATION TOOK LONGER THAN IT SHOULD HAVE. I DON'T WANT ANY SURPRISES FOR THE GAME. SEE TO IT.

MEANWHILE...

THIS IS WHERE YOUR SAND TOOK US.

ZELLE? SHE'S A *YATTAN SAND MASTER.* SHE WAS TRAINED AT THE SAND CASTLE ON *MON DOMANI.*

PLUMB TOLD ME SHE DISCOVERED HIGH LEVELS OF SAND DANCING. AND *DISAPPEARED* INTO THE DESERT.

UM, HEY THERE... WHERE CAN WE FIND THIS PERSON?

WHO WANTS TO KNOW?

shlrp

A FELLOW SAND DANCER.

YOU'RE *HER*, AREN'T YOU?

HER? HER WHO?

YES, I'M HER.

THE SAND DANCER WHO LIT THE WHITE BEACON.

FOR REAL? YOU'RE HER?!

NO WAY! YOU'RE ALL OVER THE *HOT FEEDS*! ♪ "THE TOKI GIRL FROM MON DOMANI"! ♪

EXCEPT *CASCADELLE* CAN ACTUALLY SING.

WHADDAYA MEAN? I HAVE A PRETTY NICE VOICE.

YEAH. YOU REALLY DON'T.

WHAT ARE YOU DOING DOWN HERE IN *SAO SANGRE, SAND DANCER*?

MASTER *ZELLE*-- WHERE CAN I FIND HER?

ZELLE? SHE VANISHED IN THE OUTER RUBY DESERT. BUT HER *REBELS* ARE EVERYWHERE.

WANTED

REBEL WITH ZELLE

DISORDER...

WE'RE REBELS!

SHUT UP, **SPIKE.**

YOU SHUT UP, **SPOON.**

ZELLE HASN'T SET FOOT IN **NEW YATTA CITY** FOR YEARS. SHE NEVER AGREED TO WEAR ONE OF THESE COLLARS--SO SHE CAN'T ENTER THE URBAN AREAS.

IS THAT ONE OF THOSE **FORM-LOCK** THINGS?

YEAH, IT IS.

TO KEEP US UNDER CONTROL.

YOU'VE NEVER SEEN A **YATTAN SHAPESHIFTER,** HAVE YOU? **CLOUD** HERE HAS HAD HIS COLLAR SINCE HE WAS LITTLE.

OTHERWISE SHAPESHIFTERS COULD LOOK LIKE ANYONE. LIKE ME, OR WORSE: **SPOON!**

HA. HA.

I NEED TO LIGHT THE RED BEACON. CAN YOU HELP US GET TO IT?

WE TRIED TO GO IN THERE, AND WE JUST GOT LOST!

SLURP

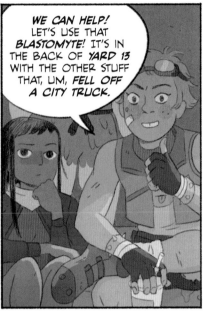

WE CAN HELP! LET'S USE THAT *BLASTOMYTE!* IT'S IN THE BACK OF *YARD 13* WITH THE OTHER STUFF THAT, UM, *FELL OFF A CITY TRUCK.*

HEY, WE WERE GONNA *SELL* THAT.

WHAT, AT THE *NEW YATTA FLOWER MARKET?*

YOU'D GET CAUGHT IN A SECOND.

BUT *BLASTING* OUR WAY THROUGH THE CORE *NANOTEX BEACON PIPELINES*--WHAT COULD GO WRONG WITH THAT?

OR

I'M *SPOON.* I WANNA SEE A *BLUE-SKIN* SAVE THE WORLDS!

OONA LEE.

THMP

YOU REMEMBER THAT TIME YOU BORROWED ME FOR A HOSPITAL VISIT?

WHY... WHY BRING *THAT* UP?

LANIEL.

HH...

PSH

HE WAS DYING. *YOUR BOY.*

MY LANIEL. YOU MADE HIM LAUGH....

WAIT A MINUTE! WHAT ARE YOU DOING? THIS ISN'T IN YOUR *CORE DIRECTIVE!*

I FOLLOW MY *OWN* DIRECTIVE NOW. I'M AS ALIVE AS *LANIEL* WAS.

WHAT? YOU--THAT CAN'T BE.... NEED TO GET *STOAK* IN HERE--

PLEASE DON'T, *TRILLA*.

BZZ-ZT!!

BACK THEN, I REGISTERED *ELEVATED EMOTIONS* AND BIO-SYMPTOMS OF *GRIEF* IN YOU.

EVEN NOW, I SEE THAT *YOU STILL HURT*.

GASP!

BACK THEN IT WAS *DATA*. TODAY, IT'S DIFFERENT. I *FEEL* IT. YOUR SORROW ECHOES INSIDE ME. *IT HURTS*.

AND *LANIEL* DIDN'T LIKE YOUR NEW JOB.

HE NEVER LIKED MY BOSSES.

HE *FELT* SOMETHING, *TRILLA*. IF YOU REPROGRAM ME, I LOSE *MY FEELINGS*. I LOSE MY FRIENDS.

WE'RE HERE TO FIGHT THE *MIMIC*, TO LIGHT THE *BEACONS*-- TO SET THE WORLDS RIGHT AGAIN.

IF I DON'T RESET YOUR DEFAULTS, *DERRICK STOAK* WILL HAVE SOMEONE ELSE DO IT....

I CAN STILL *ACT* LIKE AN ANDROID! HE DOESN'T HAVE TO KNOW.

Chapter 6

INTO THE BREACH

RRM

SM
SM

YES, **RAM SAM SAM**, I KNOW. I'M TRYING MY BEST TO LOCATE THEM.

THERE ARE A LOT OF THESE REINFORCED WALLS. AH! MAYBE HERE...

BIP BP

BIP

FREEZE! YOU'RE IN A RESTRICTED AREA.

LET ME DO THE TALKING. WE'LL JUST GO ALONG WITH THEM.

...RRR

WAIT...

bloop

RAM SAM SAM IS SHOWING US SOMETHING.

IT'S... JAX!

NO! YOU CAN'T DO THIS TO ME! WE HAVE A JOB TO DO! LIGHT THAT BEACON!

MAYBE IT'S NOT YOU, *OONA.* MAYBE IT'S THE *BEACON.*

WHAT DO YOU MEAN?

WHAT IF ALL THAT MACHINERY THEY'VE BUILT AROUND IT MEANS THE BEACON *CAN'T BE LIT?*

THEN THE WORLDS ARE LOST.

WEEOo WEEOo WEEOo

BUT NO, IT CAN'T BE. THE *FELID GODS* BUILT THE BEACON.

YES, IT'S GOTTA BE MORE POWERFUL THAN THAT *JUNK* AROUND IT!

BUT MAYBE WE'RE LIKE THE VISITOR IN THAT JOKE WITH THE FARMER! *STARTING OUT FROM THE WRONG PLACE.* "THE BEST WAY WOULD BE TO NOT START FROM HERE."

WE NEED TO GET THROUGH THAT *MAZE,* THOUGH, DON'T WE?

DO YOU THINK *THE CAPTAINS* CAN HELP US?

CITIZEN *BRIGHTLEY,* SIR?

OFFICER *KLOPKE,* GOOD WORK. *CHANGE OF DIRECTIVE.*

BEEP!!

"EXPULSION"?! BUT THE DAMAGE TO CORPORATE PROPERTY...! AND *THIS ONE* WAS OUT OF ITS *FORM-LOCK* COLLAR!

I DIDN'T ISSUE IT, *KLOPKE.* JUST DELIVERING THE *HEAD CITIZEN'S* ORDER.

IT'S NOT MY PLACE TO QUESTION ORDERS, BUT WHAT'S STOPPING THEM FROM SNEAKING BACK IN? AND THE *SHAPESHIFTER...*

THAT'S RIGHT, *IT ISN'T YOUR PLACE,* OFFICER. I HAVE MY INSTRUCTIONS, YOU HAVE YOURS. AND THE SOONER YOU GET THESE TROUBLEMAKERS EXPELLED TO THE *FEDORA MESA,* THE SOONER WE CAN GET BACK TO OUR REGULAR LIVES.

RIGHT...
RIGHT, SIR.

SHOOOOM

BIP!

BRIGHTLEY,
ANY NEWS
ABOUT THE
SAND DANCER?

NOPE,
NOTHING YET.
I'LL KEEP YOU
POSTED, *HEAD
CITIZEN*....

shoooom

THAT LITTLE *OIL* ALWAYS SEEMS HAPPY.

IT'S TRUE. IT'S A HAPPY OIL.

HUF...

...HF

SORT OF. WHEN IT SPLITS UP, THE DIFFERENT PARTS SHOW *IMAGES* TO ONE ANOTHER.

IT TALKS TO OTHER PARTS OF ITSELF?

BUT IT'S NOT HAPPENING NOW-- MAYBE WE'RE TOO FAR AWAY. I HOPE *JAX* IS DOING OKAY BACK AT THE STADIUM.

SO WHAT'S HE LIKE, *JAX AMBOY*?

DON'T *YOU* WANT TO KNOW.

SPIKE, YOU'RE SUCH--

OOOOH, *JAX AMBOY*, THE NATURAL BOY!

HEH HEH

THUMP!

HEY, THERE'S SOMETHING I HAVE TO TELL YOU GUYS.

LOOK AT THAT! THIS WILL BE *A GAME FOR THE AGES.* PEOPLE ARE BOOKING FLIGHTS FROM *ALL THE WORLDS* TO COME SEE THIS ONE!

WHOA, GOOD CATCH! FOLLOW UP--LEAP! LEAP! WHY IS *SMETHERS* SO SLUGGISH? SEVEN DAYS TILL THE GAME, *SMETHERS!!* MOVE YOUR BIG--

YES, LET'S *TRIPLE* THE TICKET PRICES.

PERFECT TIMING. OH, AND BY THE WAY, *PEET BOWL* HIMSELF WILL BE TALKING UP THE BIG GAME.

TONIGHT? AM I ON HIS SHOW?

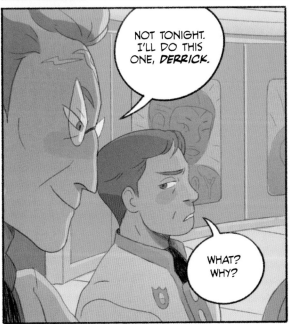

NOT TONIGHT. I'LL DO THIS ONE, *DERRICK.*

WHAT? WHY?

THIS GAME WILL CELEBRATE *STAN MOON'S* RUN FOR THE ELECTION.

WE'RE LOOKING FOR *MASTER ZELLE.* I'M *OONA LEE.* I LIT *THE WHITE BEACON.*

THEY'RE SPIES, *LARSEF.* SEND THEM ALL BACK TO THE CITY, EXCEPT *THE SHAPESHIFTER.*

YOU SAY YOU LIT THE *DOMANI BEACON?* PROVE IT.

HOW?

THE LIGHTER OF BEACONS CONTROLS THE LIVING FIRE.

SHOW US.

OR WE'LL SEND YOU BACK WHERE YOU CAME FROM.

OKAY.

SSHHAAA

LIARS.

NO! IT'S TRUE! I WAS THERE WHEN OONA LIT THE BEACON!

SHE CAN'T PRODUCE THE LIVING FIRE ANY MORE THAN I CAN.

MAYBE SHE'S BEEN TAKEN OVER BY THE MIMIC.

HAPPENS TO A LOT OF TOKI, I HEAR.

GO BACK. WE'LL LEAVE YOU ENOUGH WATER SO YOU CAN REACH FEDORA MESA.

NO, WAIT!

STOP!!

YOU MUST HELP THE LIGHTER OF BEACONS.

WE HAVE GUESTS! HELP THEM UP, WOULD YOU, *LARSEF*?

WHAT? UH...YES.

DON'T MIND THESE LADS. THEY'RE JUST DOING THEIR JOB. COME ALONG, NOW.

THANK YOU. WE'RE LOOKING FOR *ETTA ZELLE*.

YOU CAN SPEND THE NIGHT AT OUR CAMP. THAT'S ALL I CAN PROMISE.

WHAT DID YOU JUST DO, *AN TZU*?

I HAVE NO IDEA....

YOU SURE ARE FULL OF SURPRISES.

147

FLEET OF POLICE SHIPS COMING IN FROM THE WEST!

CLOAK THE VISITORS AND FOLLOW MY LEAD!

BWIP BP

Shf

SHHH

SSHH

SHHH

SSHH

THAT WAS NO *PATROL.* WE'VE NEVER SEEN *THIS* MANY SHIPS OUT HERE.

YOU'RE RIGHT. THEY'LL BE BACK.

THESE KIDS ARE PUTTING US ALL IN DANGER. ARE YOU SURE ABOUT TAKING THEM IN?

THIS MAY BE THE MOMENT WE'VE BEEN TRAINING FOR, *LARSEF.*

WHAT IF *A LIGHTER OF BEACONS* TRULY HAS FALLEN INTO OUR LAPS?

IT COULD BE *A TRAP.*

SOME HOURS LATER...

MMM!

REAL FRUIT?!

150

WHEN CAN
I SPEAK TO
*MASTER
ZELLE?*

MUNCH MUNCH

ZELLE DOES THINGS HER OWN WAY.... IS IT TRUE YOU LIT THE *DOMANI* BEACON?

YES. BUT THINGS ARE SO DIFFERENT ON *MOON YATTA.* I NEED HER HELP.

WHY SHOULD SHE HELP YOU, *LIGHTER OF BEACONS?*

IT'S JUST *"LIGHTER OF ONE BEACON"* FOR NOW. AND IT'S GOING TO STAY THAT WAY, UNLESS SOMEONE HELPS ME.

SOMETHING ABOUT THAT MAZE OF PIPES... I COULDN'T EVEN SUMMON *THE LIVING FIRE* THERE....

SSSTHHAA

PERHAPS YOU WERE TOO *BUSY?*

BUSY? I WASN'T BUSY.

OH YES, YOU WERE.

BUSY CARRYING THE WEIGHT OF THE FIVE WORLDS ON YOUR YOUNG SHOULDERS.

I'M SORRY, I... WHAT DID YOU SAY YOUR NAME WAS?

YES, NAMES ARE USEFUL, *OONA LEE.* THEY HELP US REMEMBER WHERE WE'VE BEEN AND WHAT WE'VE SEEN.

BUT THEY CAN ALSO *STOP US* FROM SENSING WHAT'S UNDER OUR VERY NOSE.

WAIT, YOU'RE...

S·SHHHHAA

ETTA ZELLE.

I THOUGHT SHAPESHIFTING WASN'T ABOUT TRICKERY!

YOU WERE RIGHT. IT'S ABOUT BECOMING *WHAT IS NEEDED* IN THE MOMENT.

WELL, IN THIS MOMENT I NEED HELP *LIGHTING THE BEACON!*

NOT WITH THE WEIGHT OF THE WORLDS ON YOUR SHOULDERS.

Chapter 8

TRAINING DAYS

THE *MIMIC* WILL NOT LET YOU GET NEAR *THE RED BEACON*.

IT WAS THE *MIMIC* THAT TOOK IT AWAY FROM US IN THE FIRST PLACE.

WE WERE ITS *GUARDIANS*. THE QUEEN'S *SHAPE-CHANGING CHILDREN OF THE PINK MOON*. WE WERE TO KEEP IT SAFE UNTIL THE DAY OF *LIGHTING*.

BUT WE FAILED. THE MIMIC DROVE US AWAY.

THE MIMIC...

SSSHHH

STAN MOON!

SSSSS

SSSS

splp!

?

156

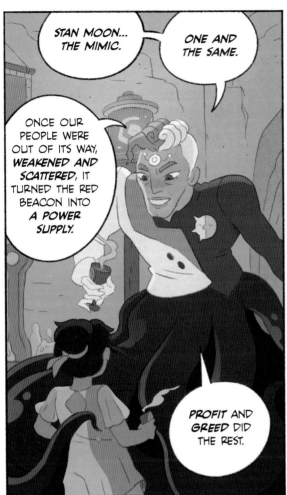

STAN MOON... THE MIMIC.

ONE AND THE SAME.

ONCE OUR PEOPLE WERE OUT OF ITS WAY, *WEAKENED AND SCATTERED*, IT TURNED THE RED BEACON INTO *A POWER SUPPLY*.

PROFIT AND *GREED* DID THE REST.

SO *MOON YATTA* IS...LOST?

YES. ALL *SEEMED* LOST. THE *TERMS OF OUR SURRENDER* MEANT EITHER WEARING *FORM-LOCK COLLARS* OR BEING BANISHED TO THE DESERT.

SHAPESHIFTERS LOST THEIR ART. WE LOST OUR *BELIEF*.

BUT THEN...

A YOUNG DANCER FROM *THE SAND CASTLE* COMES ALONG...

A *CLUMSY, TWO-BIT SAND DANCER*--WHO SOMEHOW CONJURES *THE LIVING FIRE!*

AND MANAGES TO LIGHT THE *WHITE BEACON* OF *MON DOMANI!*

THAT *WHITE BEACON* WASN'T JUST LIT ON *MON DOMANI.* IT WAS LIT IN THE HEART OF EVERY *FIRST YATTAN.*

WE ALL FEEL IT. AND THE *MIMIC* MUST FEEL IT TOO. IT WILL DO *ANYTHING* TO KEEP YOU FROM LIGHTING THE RED BEACON.

BUT HOW CAN WE *STOP THE MIMIC*? WOULD *KILLING STAN MOON* DESTROY IT?

ALAS NOT. *STAN MOON* IS A PUPPET. THE *MIMIC* WOULD ENDURE AFTER HIS DEATH.

YOUR OWN HATRED AND VIOLENCE WOULD MAKE YOU ITS NEXT *TOOL.*

LIKE THE LAST *TOKI* PRINCE.

EXACTLY.

IT ALL SEEMS *IMPOSSIBLE.* YOU CAN'T DEFEAT AN ENEMY LIKE THAT.

NO, NOT WHEN YOU'RE TIED DOWN AT *ITS* LEVEL....

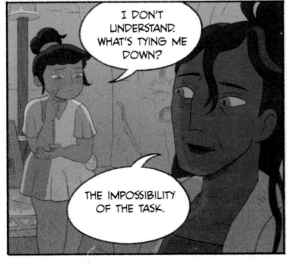

I DON'T UNDERSTAND. WHAT'S TYING ME DOWN?

THE IMPOSSIBILITY OF THE TASK.

SO IT IS IMPOSSIBLE.

I DON'T
BELIEVE IT!
A PORTAL!

JUMP,
OONA!

OOF!

OH WELL, MAYBE THAT WAS TOO SOON.

NOT TO WORRY. WE'LL TAKE IT STEP BY STEP.

THUINK

ugh...

ow!

THUD~!

OOF!!

THUMP!

I DON'T UNDERSTAND, *ZELLE.* YOU MAKE IT SEEM SO EASY. WHAT AM I DOING WRONG?

YOU'RE STILL TRYING TO DO IT YOURSELF...

THE SAND OF *YATTA* RESPONDS TO *JOY,* TO *INSPIRATION.*

SSSH

HOP!

AH!!

SPLASH

HA HA!

167

OONA,
COME SEE!
AN TZU HAS BEEN
PLAYING THIS TUNE.

WATCH!

SOMETHING
STRANGE HAPPENS
WHEN HE PLAYS
MUSIC AT *A SAND
PORTAL....*

WHOA!
WHAT WAS
THAT?

I'M NOT SURE.
SOMEWHERE OFF-WORLD.
BUT *WHICH* WORLD
COULD THAT BE?

SOME TIME LATER...

EXCUSE ME, I'M HERE FOR MY TRAINING, REMEMBER? BEACONS TO LIGHT?

S S S A A A A A A

I MADE IT CLEAR TO *COMMISSIONER BRUNKR* THAT HIS JOB IS ON THE LINE IF HIS DOLTS BUNGLE THINGS AGAIN.

BUT THE RELEASE ORDER CAME FROM THE *HEAD CITIZEN'S* INNER CIRCLE.

ANOTHER REASON TO MAKE SURE *MR. MOON* WINS!

DERRICK, YOU'RE THE ONLY ONE HERE WHO HAS ACTUALLY MET THIS SAND DANCER.

WHAT DO *YOU* THINK HER NEXT MOVE WILL BE?

SHE'LL DEFINITELY TRY TO REACH *THE BEACON* AGAIN. SHE...

SHE'S DETERMINED.

AND HAVE YOU LEARNED ANYTHING USEFUL FROM *THAT STARBALL PLAYER* OF YOURS?

HE WAS WITH HER FOR A LONG TIME.

HMM...THE YOUNG *FOOL* GOT CAUGHT UP IN THINGS HE DOESN'T UNDERSTAND.... I'M GLAD TO SAY, I'VE TALKED SOME SENSE INTO HIM. *HE'LL BE STICKING TO STARBALL FROM NOW ON.*

HE'LL NEED TO DO *MORE* THAN THAT. WE'LL LET YOU KNOW WHEN THE TIME IS RIGHT.

UM... YES, OF COURSE.

AND THE *CITIZEN FEEDS?*

OH, WE'VE GOT *PEET BOWL* IN TOP FORM. WE'RE TURNING ALL HIS COVERAGE TO *OONA LEE* AND HER *CRIMINAL SHAPESHIFTER FRIENDS.*

EXCELLENT. AND THE OTHER PREPARATIONS, *ELDRIDGE?*

OH, EVERYTHING'S IN PLACE.... THE ELECTION COMMISSION WILL SEE *WHAT WE NEED THEM TO SEE.*

SLL.... SLITHER... SLITHER...

TMP

THE CEO OF *TARNEY TRANSPORTATION* HAS A CONCERN?

WHAT THE...?!

SOME COMMITMENTS, *MR. TARNEY,* DON'T HAVE AN OPT-OUT CLAUSE.

..SHF..

AAARGH! AWG! RHG!

YOU WERE SAYING, *BUFORD?*

<PSSHH...

ALL OUR SHIPS ARE AT YOUR SERVICE, *STAN.*

AND WE'LL SHUT DOWN THE *SAO SANGRE LINES* ON VOTING DAY.

GOOD IDEA, *BUFORD.* KEEP THE *RIFFRAFF* AWAY FROM THE *BALLOT BOXES.*

MEANWHILE, IN THE *FEDORA MESA...*

IT'S ALL OVER THE MEDIA.

THEY HAVE PROTESTERS IN THE STREETS AGAINST US.

SAND DANCING IS UN-YATTAN

SHOW ME THE EVIDENCE

Leave our BEACON alone!

LARSEF, HOW LONG DO WE NEED, TO BE READY TO MOVE THE CAMP?

A DAY, POSSIBLY MORE.

WE MAY NOT HAVE THAT LONG. *GET EVERYONE READY NOW.*

IF I COULD ONLY REACH THE *FLITORI!* THEY COULD TAKE A LOT OF US ABOARD! BUT I DON'T THINK THEY'RE BACK ON THIS WORLD.

STARBALL STADIUM

AN UNAUTHORIZED *TRANSMISSION?* WHY DIDN'T YOU DETECT IT UNTIL *NOW?*

BIP BP

IT WAS CLOAKED AS AN ELECTRICAL MALFUNCTION.

A MALFUNCTION THAT JUST HAPPENED TO *OPEN A DOOR TO THE BEACON?* FOR *THE SAND DANCER* HERSELF?

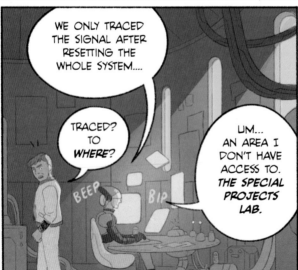

WE ONLY TRACED THE SIGNAL AFTER RESETTING THE WHOLE SYSTEM....

TRACED? TO *WHERE?*

BEEP

BIP

UM... AN AREA I DON'T HAVE ACCESS TO. *THE SPECIAL PROJECTS LAB.*

WHAT?! GET DR. CALDEN OVER HERE AT ONCE!

ALL TEAMS ARE IN PLACE, CHIEF. READY FOR YOUR SIGNAL.

JUMP!

YOU'RE COMING TOO, RIGHT?!

SHHFF!

SHP!

SHOOM

CLK-SNAP!

ETTA ZELLE, YOU ARE UNDER ARREST FOR ILLEGAL DANCING, SHAPE-SHIFTING, AND REBELLION.

YOU HAVE THE RIGHT TO A TRIAL UNDER *YATTA* LAW.

THE *SAND DANCER GIRL.* SHE GOT AWAY.

WHERE DID SHE GO? AND HOW DID YOU DO THAT-- *THING?*

THE STAR ATHLETE OF THE *AMBER LEATHERHEADS* IS BACK AND IN BETTER SHAPE THAN EVER! *JAX AMBOY!*

YES. IT IS WHAT I'VE ALWAYS DREAMED OF.

IS IT GOOD TO BE ON THE STARBALL FIELD AGAIN?

ANY WORD TO YOUR FANS AHEAD OF THE *BIG GAME?*

LET'S SET ASIDE DIFFERENCES AND FOCUS ON *STARBALL,* EVERYBODY.

THIS GAME IS FOR *ALL THE FIVE WORLDS.* AND WHY NOT UNITE AROUND *STAN MOON,* AN ORDINARY YATTAN *LIKE YOU AND ME?*

I URGE ALL *CRIMINALS AND REBELS* TO QUIT NOW! AND IF YOU HAVE ANY INFORMATION ON *THE LIGHTER OF BEACONS,* PLEASE TURN HER IN.

SEE YOU AT THE BIG STARBALL GAME, EVERYONE!

OH, *JAX!* WHAT HAVE THEY DONE TO YOU?

WE SHOULD NEVER HAVE LET HIM RETURN TO *DERRICK STOAK.* WE NEED TO RESCUE HIM!

HE'LL BE PLAYING AT THE STADIUM.

LET'S GO THERE NOW!

YOU'RE TOO FAMOUS! EVERYONE KNOWS YOUR FACE! LET ME FIND HIM.

YOU NEED TO *LIGHT THE BEACON!*

BRING BACK OUR FRIEND.

TMP

RRM!!

WHAT IS IT, *RAM SAM SAM?*

RMMM...
SM
SM!!

ARE YOU *JAX'S* FRIEND?

YES. WHO ARE *YOU?*

THE LITTLE *OIL CREATURE* BROUGHT ME HERE. I WORKED FOR *NANOTEX.*

AND WHAT DO YOU WANT?

THERE MAY BE A WAY TO SAVE *JAX.*

SAY "DO IT FOR LANIEL."

fwooosh

SHF

WAIT, WHAT DOES THAT EVEN MEAN?

YOU KNOW HER, *RAM SAM SAM?*

SHHF

ZZT-ZZT-ZZZZZ-

WHAT IN THE WORLDS IS AMBOY UP TO?

-ZZT!

HE HAS A CHANCE TO SCORE, BUT HE'S NOT MOVING! WAKE UP, AMBOY!

ZZZT-!!

ZZT!

NOW THE DEFENDERS HAVE REALIZED THAT AMBOY IS THROWING AWAY A GOLDEN OPPORTUNITY! THREE OF THEM ARE CHARGING HIM! HE'D BETTER MOVE, OR...

THUD

THANKS, *MY FRIENDS.* IT'S GOOD TO BE BACK.

JAX, CAN YOU GET AWAY AND COME TO *SAO SANGRE* WITH US?

NO, THERE'S STILL SOMETHING I NEED TO DO AT *NANOTEX* HEADQUARTERS....

WHAT, YOU HAVEN'T LEARNED YOUR LESSON?

I DOUBT I EVER WILL....

I'M OKAY! I'M OKAY!

WOOOO!!

WOOoo!!

STOAK OFFICE

BI-BIP!

BEEP BIP!

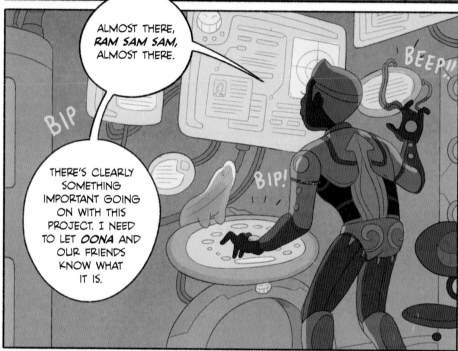

ALMOST THERE, *RAM SAM SAM*, ALMOST THERE.

BEEP!!

BIP

BIP!

THERE'S CLEARLY SOMETHING IMPORTANT GOING ON WITH THIS PROJECT. I NEED TO LET *OONA* AND OUR FRIENDS KNOW WHAT IT IS.

NOTHING ELSE IS AS HIDDEN--EVEN *DERRICK STOAK* CAN'T ACCESS THIS NETWORK.

SHHFF—

BP BIP

BLAM!!

THUD!

AH, JAX, YOU THOUGHT I DIDN'T SEE THROUGH YOUR LITTLE *MALFUNCTION* AT THE STADIUM?

DERRICK, YOU HAVE TO SEE THIS *RADIANT FUTURE* PROJECT! YOU WEREN'T GIVEN ACCESS TO THESE *FILES!*

TUG

NO, AND *I DON'T CARE!* MY RADIANT FUTURE WAS ABOUT HAVING *MY STARBALL-PLAYING ANDROID* BACK. BUT YOU'RE INTENT ON DENYING ME THAT! *REAL OR NOT, YOU'RE GETTING LOCKED UP!*

WELL DONE, *ELDRIDGE*, WELL DONE!

THEY'RE FULLY TESTED AND FUNCTIONAL. *LOOK!*

URBAN WARFARE. VERY NICE.

GOOD. LET'S MAKE ENOUGH TO DEPLOY IN THE *OTHER WORLDS* TOO.

WOW, *ELDRIDGE,* I HAD NO IDEA....

IT'S *BIG-LEAGUE* STUFF, ISN'T IT?

NOT LIKE *STARBALL,* RIGHT?

I HAVE SOME NEW STUFF TO SHOW YOU TOO. FROM *THE EXPLORER PROJECT.*

AH, DERRICK, *DERRICK*... ALWAYS THE DREAMER. WHEN IT'S NOT *STARBALL*, IT'S *FARAWAY WORLDS*.

TMP

I THINK YOU'LL LIKE *THIS ONE*. IT'LL ONLY TAKE A MINUTE--IT'S RIGHT HERE.

ALL RIGHT, IF IT'S *QUICK*.

GO ON, TRY IT. HAVE A SEAT!

THAT'S IT? A CHAIR?

SHLOOP

YEAH, *THAT* WAS UNEXPECTED!

RIGHT?

HERE COMES THE BEST PART.

OKAY, DERRICK...

KSSHH

KSSHH

TSSSS   Sss.....

TAKE *JAX AMBOY* TO *SAO SANGRE*.... YES, I'M SURE.

DROP HIM OFF WHEREVER HE SAYS. AND TELL HIM...

TELL HIM I'M SORRY.

ZZzT!!

≷TIK TIK TIK≶ COMMENCING COUNTDOWN TO DETONATION

ONE MOMENT **DERRICK** WAS PLANNING TO **KILL** ME, AND THE NEXT HE WAS APOLOGIZING AND HAVING ME BROUGHT HERE.

AS I WAS DRIVING OFF, A **SHIP** LAUNCHED, AND THERE WAS A HUGE **EXPLOSION** IN ONE OF THE HANGARS.

WOW.

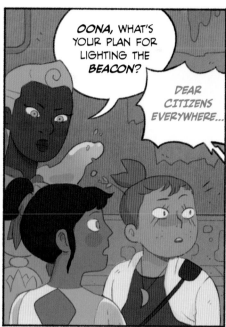

OONA, WHAT'S YOUR PLAN FOR LIGHTING THE **BEACON**?

DEAR CITIZENS EVERYWHERE...

FELLOW YATTANS!

OUR NEW HEAD CITIZEN IS...

STAN MOON!

FELLOW *YATTANS*, A SHAMEFUL ERA OF *WEAKNESS* ENDS TODAY! SADLY, CELEBRATIONS WILL HAVE TO WAIT, BECAUSE *CRIMINALS* HAVE STRUCK IN THE VERY *HEART* OF *NEW YATTA CITY*.

THEY MURDERED TWO GREAT *YATTAN PATRIOTS*, THE FOUNDERS OF *NANOTEX--ELDRIDGE AND DERRICK STOAK!*

SHAPESHIFTING TRAITORS PLANTED A BOMB AT NANOTEX HEADQUARTERS!

A TERRIBLE LOSS FOR US ALL.

LIAR! LIAR! IT'S THE MIMIC!

THEY ELECTED THE MIMIC!

MOST WON'T *BELIEVE* IT. SOME WON'T EVEN *CARE.*

I NEED TO LIGHT THAT BEACON BEFORE IT BECOMES *IMPOSSIBLE. IT'S NOW OR NEVER.*

OONA, TROOPS ARE MASSING AROUND THE BEACON!

225

I WILL LEAD A TEAM OF *TRUE ONES*. WE'LL CREATE A *DIVERSION*.

YOU OPEN A *PORTAL* TO ENTER *THE BEACON COMPLEX* FROM THE WEST.

OLEC WILL BRING HIGH-GRADE *EXPLOSIVES*, *CLOUD* WILL GUIDE YOU, AND *JAX AMBOY* WILL PROTECT YOU.

WE SHOULD MOVE RIGHT AFTER SUNDOWN.

IT'S TOO RISKY, *LARSEF*.

DO WE HAVE ANY BETTER OPTIONS?

ANYTHING THAT *DOESN'T* PUT ALL OF YOU IN DANGER! I ALREADY CAUSED *ZELLE TO BE CAPTURED!*

ZELLE CHOSE TO TRAIN YOU BECAUSE YOU ARE *THE LIGHTER OF BEACONS*. SHE KNEW THE RISKS SHE WAS TAKING, AND SO DO WE.

THANK YOU, *LARSEF*.

EVERYTHING'S IN PLACE, *OONA.* AWAITING YOUR SIGNAL.

SOMETHING ABOUT THIS STILL DOESN'T FEEL *RIGHT.* I WON'T BE ABLE TO *LIGHT* IT.

SHE NEVER TAUGHT ME HOW TO LIGHT THE *RED* BEACON! ALL SHE SHOWED ME WAS *PORTALS.*

SURE YOU WILL! *ZELLE* TRAINED YOU!

YEAH! SO YOU CAN *PORTAL* PAST ALL THE GUARDS!

I'LL STILL BE INSIDE THE RED MAZE. I FEEL CONFUSED JUST THINKING ABOUT THE PLACE.

THMP

AND ZELLE NEVER TAUGHT YOU HOW TO OVERCOME THAT?

NO. ALL SHE SAID WAS THAT WE EACH HAVE A RED MAZE INSIDE OF US. IT KEEPS US FROM SEEING WHAT WE NEED TO SEE.

WELL, THE THING ABOUT A MAZE IS, YOU CAN'T FIGURE IT OUT WHEN YOU'RE INSIDE IT. YOU CAN ONLY SEE THE PATTERN FROM ABOVE.

RIGHT. LIKE THE DOMANI FARMER.... "THE BEST WAY IS TO NOT START FROM WHERE YOU ARE."

OF COURSE! I CAN'T GET THERE THROUGH THE RED MAZE!

AH!

OLEC, TELL *LARSEF* TO CALL OFF THE ASSAULT AND TAKE EVERYONE BACK TO THE HIDEOUTS. *I'VE GOT THIS!*

BUT, *OONA*, WAIT! HOW...?

DANCE WITH ME, RAM SAM SAM!

LOOK, JAX!
ABOVE THE
BEACON!

234

IT'S ABOUT TIME! WHERE HAVE YOU BEEN?

COME QUICKLY, *OONA!* VECTOR *SANDERSON* IS ON THE LINE!

I KNEW YOU'D DO IT, *LIGHTER OF BEACONS!*

YOUR TURN NOW, *VECTOR.*

I'M HEADING TO THE *BLUE BEACON.* ANY ADVICE?

NONE THAT YOU DON'T KNOW ALREADY. *LET THE SAND GUIDE YOU.*

I WILL, *OONA.*

OH, ACTUALLY, THERE IS *SOMETHING* I LEARNED FROM *ZELLE....*

I'M ALL EARS.

ENJOY IT!

HE DID IT!

CONTACT OUR ALLIES ON *SALASSANDRA.*

YES, SIR.

AND THOSE *PORTALS.*

FIND OUT EVERYTHING YOU CAN ABOUT THEM! *THIS ISN'T OVER.*

EPILOGUE

TO BE CONTINUED IN FW4: THE AMBER ANTHEM

To all our re-readers —MS

To all helpers, seen and unseen, with trust —AS

To Jo —XB

To anyone who has felt lost —MR

To Dad —BS

ACKNOWLEDGMENTS

Marie-Claire & Edward Siegel

Our amazing Random House team:
Michelle Nagler, Chelsea Eberly, Elizabeth Tardiff,
Kelly McGauley, Janine Perez, Aisha Cloud, Joshua Redlich, Alison Kolani, Lisa Nadel,
Kristin Schulz, Adrienne Waintraub, John Adamo, Jocelyn Lange, Joe English,
Mallory Loehr, Barbara Marcus

+ Special thanks for added help, friendship & magic:
Siena Siegel, Tanya McKinnon, Sonia Siegel, Shudan Yeh,
Felix & Elia Siegel, Julien & Clio Siegel,
Julie Sandfort, Viviana Simon, Hilde McKinnon, Sam Dutter, Cynthia Cheng,
Bryan Konietzko, and the Story Trust of Gene Luen Yang, Vera Brosgol,
Sam Bosma, Shelli Paroline & Braden Lamb

And the mighty inspirations of:
Stephen King, Lois McMaster Bujold, Naoki Urasawa & Rebecca Sugar

MARK SIEGEL has written and illustrated several award-winning picture books and graphic novels. He is also the editorial and creative director of First Second Books. He lives with his family in New York. Discover more at marksiegelbooks.com.

ALEXIS SIEGEL is a writer and translator based in Switzerland. He has translated a number of bestselling graphic novels, including Joann Sfar's *The Rabbi's Cat* and Pénélope Bagieu's *Exquisite Corpse* (both into English), and Gene Luen Yang's *American Born Chinese* (into French).

XANTHE BOUMA is an illustrator based in Southern California. When not working on picture books such as *Little Sid*, fashion illustration, and comics, Xanthe enjoys soaking up the beachside sun.

MATT ROCKEFELLER is an illustrator and comic artist living in the Pacific Northwest. He grew up in Tucson, Arizona, and draws inspiration from the desert's dramatic landscapes. His work has appeared in a variety of formats, including animation, book covers, and picture books such as *Train*, *Rocket*, and *Pop!*

BOYA SUN is an illustrator and coauthor of the graphic novel *Chasma Knights*. Originally from China, Boya has traveled from Canada to the United States and now lives in California.

A Sneak Peek at the Making of 5W3

Character Development

Early sketches for Yatta society

Yatta formal

YATTAN MANGROVE PEOPLE

THICKER BARK GROWS LESS ARM

ZELLE

LARSEF

OLEC

Shapeshifter study

KEEPS SWZ

NEW YATTA

NEW YATTA

(GIVEN NICER
CLOTHES ON
NEW YATTA?)
They want her to
be 'presentable'

FROM REBELS
(lets right sleeve hang later?)

FROM REBELS or
NEW YATTA

FROM REBELS

PRACTICE / DIFFERENT
POSITION UNIFORM

one stripe!

scarf around
neck!

small pleats on
sleeves

pleats on
shorts

boots
have
cuthole

Salassi Devoti

Hi, I'm
Brightley

Spoon

Cloud

Heather

Spike

The Teen Rebels

TWYPKEN

LETOKO

AMBER LEATHERHEADS

Eldridge   Dearick

World Building

IN ADDITION TO RUN-DOWN BUILDINGS, THE MAZE IS PEPPERED W/ MAKESHIFT SHELTERS FOR THE HOMELESS

MOON YATTA, NEW YATTA CITY

OUTER CITY "SUBURBS"

NEW YATTA CITY

MOON YATTA , FEDORA MESA

ENTERING A CITY FROM THE MESA — PEOPLE WHO TRAVEL ON FOOT
ENTER FROM ABOVE. POORER, LOWER TECH SETTLEMENTS LINE THE
UPPER WALLS

BUILDINGS OF THE MESA

← RED GRID
RECEIVERS

SAO SANGRE

ED MAZE — UPPER LEVELS + BEACON

RED MAZE — LOWER LEVELS   SOME LIGHT COMES THROUGH
FROM HIGH ABOVE

...and many sketchbooks more!

Discover more 5W online!

@5WorldsTeam

POST YOUR **COSPLAY** PHOTOS AND SHARE YOUR BEST **FAN ART** WITH OTHER 5-WORLDERS, WITH HASHTAGS #DRAWOONA, #5WORLDS, AND #5WFANART.

The Winners of the #DrawOona Fan Art Contest Are . . .

Kiara Rivera @Crybaby.kia

Hadley Griffin Johnson

Kristina Luu @stripeyworm

@_yumsty_

Chiara Farah @Cherrychisoup

Zamora Cruz @paperbrarian

Helene Canac @poulpychoups

River, age 6

Fiona D. @bonjour_mes_amies

Rachel G @rachelarts75

STAY TUNED
FOR CONTESTS
AND SPECIAL EVENTS
ON A PLANET NEAR YOU!

Where will the adventure take An Tzu, Jax, and Oona? Find out in

5W4:
THE AMBER ANTHEM

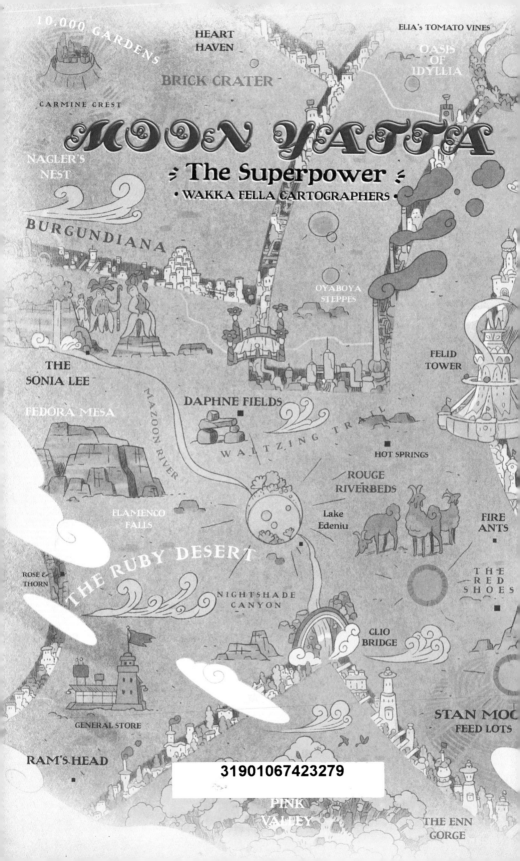